P.J. CLOVER · PRIVATE EYE
The Case of the Stolen Laundry

For Kathy —
Happy reading!
Susan Meyer

P. J. CLOVER · PRIVATE EYE

The Case of the Stolen Laundry

by Susan Meyers

Fawcett Columbine · New York

A Fawcett Columbine Book
Published by Ballantine Books
Copyright © 1981 by Susan Meyers

Library of Congress Catalog Card Number: 89-90894

ISBN: 0-449-90457-1

Cover design by Bill Geller
Cover illustration by Joel Iskowitz

Manufactured in the United States of America

First Ballantine Books Edition: March 1990

10 9 8 7 6 5 4 3 2 1

For Sue Alexander,
good writer . . . true friend

Contents

1

The Eye

It all started with the eye.

We found it—or rather, P. J. found it—sticking out of a trash bin in the alley behind Dr. Rothman's eye, ear, nose, and throat clinic.

We were on our bikes riding home from school. (We always ride home through the alleys on Thursdays since that's trash collection day, and P. J.—naturally—likes to see what she can find.)

Well, the moment she saw the eye, she skidded to a stop. Her face lit up. Her eyes sparkled. Her cheeks glowed. And her nose began to twitch like a rabbit's.

I knew that sparkle.

I knew that glow.

I knew that twitch.

And seeing them all together made goosebumps pop out on my arms. There was no doubt about it. P. J. Clover had an idea!

In a flash, she jumped from her bike and pounced on the trash. "This is it, Stacy!" she exclaimed, as she pulled the eye from the rubbish and held it up. "Exactly what we need!"

I stared.

I didn't know what she was talking about.

The big piece of white posterboard with a picture of an eye printed smack in the center didn't mean a thing to me.

But P. J. didn't stop to explain.

"This will show him," she said as she shoved the eye under the carrier rack on her bike. "This will really show him!"

"Who?" I asked. "What? Show who what?"

But it was no use. P. J. was already speeding away down the alley.

I hopped on my bike and followed. There was no point trying to make her wait. When P. J. Clover has one of her ideas, she doesn't stop for anything!

But maybe *I'd* better stop.

Pretty soon a lot of things are going to start happening and then there won't be time. Time to fill in the details, I mean. Details about who I am and who P. J. is and where we are and all that.

First me.

(P. J., of course, would want me to start with her, but there are some places where *I'm* in charge and this is one of them.)

Anyway, my name is Stacy Jones. I'm ten and a half years old and I'm in the fifth grade at Park School. I've got brown hair and brown eyes—kind of ordinary looking, I guess—and I'm a writer. I have a way with words. At least that's what Mrs. Crane our creative writing teacher says, so it must be true.

2

She also says a writer needs to have all kinds of interesting experiences. But that's no problem. Being P. J. Clover's best friend may not be easy, but it *is* interesting. And we do have experiences. Lots of them.

Which brings me to P. J. herself.

It's not easy to describe P. J. I don't mean how she looks. That's simple enough. She's tall—taller than most kids in the fifth grade—and sort of skinny with elbows and knees that seem to stick out all over the place. She's got straggly blond hair and lots of freckles and next year she's going to have to get braces on her teeth.

But that won't matter. P. J. Clover is *not* the kind of girl who cares about how she looks. She doesn't care about what people think of her, either. Those things are important. I know because I've wasted lots of time worrying about how I look and whether I sound stupid and stuff like that.

But not P. J. She doesn't think twice about putting on socks that don't match. Or asking questions in class even if the other kids groan and say she's dumb (which she's not!). Or for that matter, rummaging through trash barrels.

(Which is good, because that's how we got half the stuff in our clubhouse.)

The reason she doesn't care, I guess, is that she doesn't have time. She's too busy *doing* things. Things like setting up a newspaper, or running a flea market, or a dog-walking service, or a backyard circus. And she never seems to worry about how things are going to turn out. (She leaves that to me!) She

3

just plunges right in. Why, if she took it into her head to walk to New York City, she'd probably start out tomorrow without giving it another thought. (See below)*

There's lots more I could say. I could tell you about the kind of sandwiches she likes to eat. (Pickle and peanut butter. Ugh!) Or about her T-shirt collection. (She has tons of them with pictures of places like Miami Beach or sayings like "Never Underestimate the Power of a Woman" printed across the front.)

But I'd better not go into all that now. Because if you're like me, you're probably wondering about that eye.

The eye that was in the trash bin.

The eye that was now on the back of P. J. Clover's bike.

I could see it flapping in the breeze as she whizzed around the corner. I followed, breathing hard, down the last block and then up the alley and through the gate into P. J.'s backyard.

She'd already dumped her bike and was heading for the garage. The piece of posterboard with the eye printed on it was tucked under her arm.

---

*I wasn't planning to have footnotes, but sometimes it's hard to fit everything in. Such as where all this is taking place. So, I'll just use this spot to say that we're in California, in a town called Mill Creek, which is near the city of San Francisco.

If you look at a map, you'll see how far that is from New York City.

And you'll understand what I mean about P. J.

"P. J. !" I yelled. "Wait!"

She didn't. Acting as if she hadn't heard me, she ducked into the garage.

"What's up?" I called. I could hear her rummaging around inside. "What's going on?"

No answer.

"Come on. Tell me."

Still no answer.

P. J. can be pretty exasperating at times. But I know how to handle her. I have a surefire method and I decided to use it now.

"Pamela Jean Clover!" I shouted.

P. J. burst out of the garage like a rocket. She was holding the square of posterboard, plus a hammer, nails, paint can, and brush. Her eyes were blazing.

"Don't call me Pamela Jean!" she exploded. "Don't *ever* call me Pamela Jean!"

"Then tell me what's going on," I said.

P. J. looked at me as if I were dimwitted. She probably thought she'd already told me. Or she thought I could read her mind. Or maybe she'd even forgotten I was there, tagging along behind her.

That's how it is when P. J. gets an idea.

But now that she saw me and heard me, her anger disappeared.

(She never stays mad for long, which is why it's O.K. for me to use her real name—which you can see she hates—when I have to.)

In a flash now, the sparkle returned to her eyes. "It's the best idea I've ever had," she declared, heading across the lawn in the direction of our clubhouse. "I'll show him. I'll really show him this time!"

5

I still didn't know *what* she was talking about, but I was beginning to have a pretty good idea about *who*. There was only one person it could be.

"Do you mean Butch?" I said. "Butch Bigelow?"

P. J. dumped her load in front of the clubhouse. "You bet I do!" she said. She began to pry the lid off the paint can. "Weirdo, creepy, smart-alecky, scuzzy Butch Bigelow!" Her words were angry, but she was smiling with a kind of wicked satisfaction. "Him and his know-it-all aunt, too!" The lid popped off the paint can, spattering P. J.'s jeans with a shower of red dots. She plunged the brush into the paint.

I was glad to have at least part of the mystery cleared up.

Butch Bigelow (who actually isn't half so bad as all that) is P. J. Clover's nemesis. That means he's her enemy. Or at least her rival. At any rate, the two of them have been bugging each other ever since nursery school days.

(I'm not sure exactly why. But I think it must have something to do with always being stuck together in alphabetical order—Bigelow, Clover, Bigelow, Clover. That, plus the fact that they both like to be boss. *And* the center of attention.)

Anyway, they just can't seem to get along. This aunt business was only the latest in a long series of arguments.

"Thinks he knows all about mysteries just because his aunt in New Jersey writes detective books. Says I couldn't solve my way out of a paper bag," P. J. muttered. "Well, I'll show him!"

She stood up, red paint dripping from her brush

like blood, and began to letter something on the club-house door.

It was her name,

P. J. CLOVER

Then, underneath, the word

PRIVATE

And then . . .

"Give me the hammer and nails," she ordered.

I did.

I wasn't about to argue. I was too curious. Curious to see what would happen next.

P. J. picked up the square of posterboard she'd fished out of Dr. Rothman's trash.

The eye stared straight out at me.

Big, bold, and unblinking.

Suddenly . . . I knew what she was going to do.

2
The Private Eye

It was a brilliant idea!

And no one but P. J. would have thought of it.

No one but P. J. would have seen that eye sticking out of the trash and imagined it hanging like this:

"Private eyes," she declared, standing back to admire her work. "That's what we're going to be. Butch

Bigelow will have to eat his words. That's what he'll have to do!"

I didn't care as much about Butch Bigelow as P. J. did. But I liked the idea of being a private eye. A vision of the two of us—P. J. and me—in trench coats and dark glasses popped into my mind.

I looked at the clubhouse door. We'd have to put my name—Stacy Jones—up there, too. (P. J. doesn't always think of things like that!) But there was lots of room under the eye.

Then suddenly I thought of something.

I dashed into the garage and found a hand drill I'd seen hanging there a week ago.

"Go inside the clubhouse," I ordered P. J.

"Why?" she asked.

"Just go," I replied. Now it was *my* turn to keep *her* guessing.

She grumbled, but she went.

As soon as the door was shut, I lifted up the drill and set the bit right smack in the center of the eye. I turned the handle, and the long metal screw began to chew its way through the middle of the pupil and into the wood of the clubhouse door.

I felt the bit come out on the other side. Quickly, I screwed it back in the opposite direction and put my eye to the peephole that had been made.

P. J.'s eye looked back at me.

"Brilliant!" she said. "Absolutely brilliant!"

We tacked a piece of black cardboard over the hole on the inside. To look out, all you had to do was swivel the cardboard to one side and peek through. The hole hardly showed when the cardboard was back in place.

"Now, we'll turn this place into a headquarters," P. J. announced. She stood in the middle of the clubhouse floor and surveyed the scene.

I'd better tell you now—before going on—about our clubhouse.

It's important (and it's going to be *very* important later on) to know that it's not an ordinary clubhouse. I mean, it's not one of those things knocked together out of packing crates and old lumber. No. Definitely not. Our clubhouse is a real building.

It used to be a toolshed and it belonged to Mr. Sabatini down the block. He was going to tear it up for scrap until P. J. stopped him. She convinced him (P. J.'s very good at convincing) to give it to her instead. Then she got him to move it down the block on the back of his pickup truck and set it up on cement blocks in her backyard.

When Butch Bigelow saw it, he practically turned green with envy. And it's not hard to understand why. Besides having a door with a real lock, the clubhouse has a window that opens and shuts, and a roof that doesn't leak. Not even in the biggest storms. There's room inside for a table, some shelves, and a couple of chairs. We found an old braided rug for the floor and made steps up to the door out of more cement blocks.

We've used the clubhouse for lots of things in the past. For lots of P. J.'s big ideas, that is. It's been a rock museum, a fortune-telling booth, a boarding kennel for hamsters, rats, rabbits, etc., and now . . . it was about to be transformed into a private eye's headquarters.

"We'll have to set up some files," P. J. said as she

began to move the furniture around. "Do you think we should charge by the day or work for free like Nancy Drew?"

"That depends on the case," I said. "Some cases might be . . ."

Suddenly, I stopped. As I told you, I'm the one who usually thinks of the details that have to be ironed out before P. J.'s schemes can work, and I'd thought of a big one. Cases! What kind of cases were we going to handle?

But P. J. wasn't worried.

"There's lots of stuff going on around here," she said. "All kinds of crimes and mysteries just waiting to be solved."

That was news to me. I'd always thought Mill Creek was a pretty peaceful town. "I'm not so sure," I said. "And besides, even if there are a few mysteries lying around, what's going to make people bring them to us?"

P. J. wasn't bothered about that, either. "We'll build a reputation," she said calmly. She was sitting at the table now, cutting a piece of white construction paper into rectangles.

"One case will lead to another," she went on, taking a ball-point pen from the box of supplies we keep in the clubhouse and beginning to write on one of the rectangles. "Why, as soon as people hear about us, they'll come flocking to our door. They'll be begging us to solve their cases for them!"

"We need the first one, though," I pointed out, leaning across the table to see what she was writing. "If we don't have the first . . ."

But I didn't get to finish.

(I didn't get to see what she was writing, either. Though I certainly *did* find out later on!)

I didn't finish because all at once—right there in the middle of that peaceful block in the peaceful town of Mill Creek—the silence was suddenly broken.

Broken by no less than a hair-raising, nerve-jangling, ear-splitting *scream*!

3

"It's My Laundry"

For a second, everything seemed to stop.

It was like a movie that had come to a halt right in the middle of an exciting scene.

P. J.'s eyes opened wide and her hand froze on the pen.

My breath stopped.

And a fly, walking across the window pane, flattened itself against the glass as if in preparation for the worst.

Then suddenly, the film started moving again and everyone leaped into action. P. J. jumped up, stuffing a couple of the white rectangles into her pocket, and bounded for the door.

I came out of my trance and dashed after her.

And the fly buzzed furiously away.

By the time we burst out of the clubhouse, the screaming had stopped. For a moment, I thought maybe we'd imagined it. But then I saw old Mrs. Garrity, from the house across the alley, come flying out of her back door, a look of alarm on her face. Next, Mr. Lee came running out of his house. And I knew it had really happened.

P. J. disappeared through an opening in the tall hedge that separated her backyard from the Baxter's next door. I could hear someone on the other side of the hedge moaning.

I don't know what I expected to see as I slipped through after P. J. A body lying on the lawn maybe. But all I *did* see was Mrs. Baxter. She was standing up and she didn't look injured in any way. What had sounded like moaning now sounded like, "Oh, dear, oh dear."

"What happened, Mrs. Baxter?" P. J. asked breathlessly.

"What's going on here?" Mrs. Garrity popped through the gate leading into the backyard from the alley and looked around suspiciously.

"Are you all right?" Mr. Lee asked as he followed Mrs. Garrity through the gate. "Has anyone been hurt?"

For the first time, Mrs. Baxter seemed to become aware of the crowd that had gathered around her. She was a thin, nervous sort of woman, and now she looked embarrassed. "Oh my," she said, "I didn't mean to alarm you. I'm quite all right. It's ... it's my laundry."

I looked around the yard. I didn't see any laundry. Just an empty clothesline. P. J. and I traded glances. Was Mrs. Baxter imagining things?

She must have guessed what we were thinking,

because she quickly began to explain. "It's not there *now*, of course," she said, wringing her hands anxiously. "But it was. That's just it. I hung it on the line before I went out to my volunteer job at the library, and now it's . . . it's *gone!*"

I saw P. J.'s eyes light up. She didn't waste any time. "Have you got your notebook?" she whispered to me.

I did.

It was in my back pocket where it always is.

(As I said, I'm a writer and writers always carry notebooks around to jot down ideas.)

"Put down everything that sounds important," P. J. said in a low voice. Then, before any of the grown-ups could say a word, she turned to Mrs. Baxter. "I believe my associate and I can be of some help," she announced in a confident voice. And she pulled one of the white paper rectangles out of her pocket and handed it to Mrs. Baxter.

Mrs. Baxter looked confused. She stared at P. J. standing there in her paint-spattered blue jeans, her grubby tennis shoes, and a T-shirt with a faded can of Campbell's soup stenciled on the front. Then she looked down at the card and read what was printed on it. "P. J. Clover, Private . . ." She stopped, looking more baffled than ever.

"Eye," P. J. prompted. "Private eye."

At that point, my curiosity got the better of me and I stepped forward—along with Mrs. Garrity and Mr. Lee—to have a look.

Maybe I'd better show you what I saw:

```
P. J. CLOVER
  PRIVATE 👁
No case too large
No case too small
(Stacy Jones, associate)
 Phone 388-9456
```

It was a little embarrassing (especially when I saw the grown-ups exchange a smile of amusement) but impressive all the same.

A business card! Who but P. J. would have thought of that? This time she'd remembered to include my name, too.

Mrs. Baxter didn't laugh. After all, she'd lived next door to P. J. for years. She was used to unusual things going on beyond the hedge that separated their houses. But she did shake her head as if she thought it might be hopeless. "Thank you, P. J.," she said. "Of course, I'll be grateful for any help you can give me. But I don't know if it will come soon enough. You see, there was something very important in that laundry. Something I must have by Saturday or . . ."

But she didn't complete her sentence because just then a black and white car with a flashing red light pulled up in the alley behind the Baxter's house.

There was no mistaking who it was.

The police!

4

"May I Quote You?"

"I called them," Mr. Lee quickly explained. "Soon as I heard that scream. Thought someone was being murdered."

The door of the police car opened and a uniformed officer got out. He didn't have his gun drawn, but his hand was resting on the holster as he came through the open gate.

He took in the scene at a glance. (I guess he was expecting to see a body on the ground, too.) Then he turned slightly and motioned for a man sitting in the police car to follow him.

"What seems to be the matter here?" he asked as they crossed the lawn.

"Oh, dear," Mrs. Baxter started wringing her hands again. "The police. I've never been in trouble with the police before."

"And you're not now," P. J. pointed out. Then she took things into her own hands. "There's been a robbery here, officer," she said. "Mrs. Baxter's the *victim*, not the criminal."

The policeman looked P. J. over. His eyes rested for a minute on the paint spots (Did he think that they were blood?) and then traveled up to the Campbell's soup can. "Are you a witness?" he asked at last.

"No, but I live next door," P. J. replied. And she pulled another one of the white cards from her pocket and handed it to the policeman.

The man who had followed the officer from the car looked at the card. A grin spread slowly over his face. He took a notebook and pencil from the pocket of his sports jacket and jotted something down.

The policeman seemed at a loss for words. "Well . . ." he said. "Well . . . um . . ."

"Mind if I keep this?" the man in the sports jacket asked, reaching for the card.

"Be my guest," P. J. replied graciously.

I felt my ears getting hot and I knew I was blushing. As I said, P. J. never seems to worry about what people think of us, but *I* do. I was embarrassed by all this grown-up smiling. Embarrassed and annoyed, too. What was wrong with them, anyway? Hadn't they ever heard of enterprising youth, or in other words, kids who *do* things instead of just playing around?

Fortunately, the policeman didn't make any comment about the card. Instead, he turned to the man in the sports jacket and introduced him. "This is Fred Scott of *The Morning Gazette*. He's doing a story on the Mill Creek police. Do you mind if he listens in, ma'am?"

"Oh dear, the newspapers, too," Mrs. Baxter murmured. "Well, maybe a little publicity will help. I must have that laundry back by Saturday. I must!"

"We'll do what we can," the policeman said soothingly. "Now, why don't you begin at the beginning. You say the theft involved laundry . . . ?"

My ears had cooled down a few degrees and now they seemed to open up wider. I didn't need P. J.'s poke in the side to realize that I'd better get this down. I'd seen enough police shows on TV to know that you had to take notes on the victim's statement. Why, we might have to testify in court or something! I flipped to a clean page in my notebook. And for the next fifteen minutes, three pencils—the policeman's, the newspaperman's, and mine, the associate private eye's—were kept busy taking down what Mrs. Baxter said.

As you can imagine, my notes were pretty messy. After all, I was writing fast and my pad of paper was small. Besides, P. J. kept poking me every few seconds to make sure I was getting the important stuff down.

But I copied them over, organized them, and checked on the spelling later on. (Now, that's the sort of thing P. J. Clover—for all her poking—would never have the patience to do!) So here they are (I think they're pretty good too):

I.	**What Mrs. Baxter did:**
1.	Put clothes in washing machine.
O	9:45 AM
2.	Hung clothes on line.
3.	Left house to go to job. 12:15 PM (clothes were online when she left. Knows because she carried garbage through backyard to alley at 12:10)
4.	Came home at 3:45 PM

5.	Went to backyard to take clothes off the line. They were gone‼
Ⅱ	What was in the laundry:
O	
1.	Assorted towels.
2.	Mr. Baxter's underwear, socks, etc.
3.	Tommy Baxter's underwear, socks, etc.
4.	2 shirts (Mr. Baxter)
5.	Blouse (Mrs. Baxter)
6.	Football uniform (Tommy)
7.	Blue jeans (Tommy)
8.	Gold-colored tea cloth embroidered with
O	chrysanthemums.

Mrs. Baxter, of course, didn't put things so simply. She spent a lot of time telling us about that garbage, for instance. About how it's really her son Tommy's job to take it out . . .

P. J. and I both know Tommy, of course. He's in the sixth grade. He's nice and he's a really good artist, too. His pictures are always hanging up in the school library. I suppose he's more interested in drawing than in dragging garbage around. (Actually, I think he's sort of frail, though he *is* on the touch football team at school. That's probably his dad's idea, though. He was some kind of college football star. A real "macho" man. I suppose he expects Tommy to be one, too.)

Anyway, Mrs. Baxter said Tommy always forgets to take out the garbage, so on Thursdays (which is trash collection day) she usually winds up taking it out because if she didn't, there would be too much the next week and it would start smelling up the kitchen, etc., etc.

But it was when she got to that gold-colored, embroidered tea cloth at the end of the list that she really carried on!

It seems that Mrs. Baxter was counting on the tea cloth to help her win first prize in the Mill Creek Garden Club's Fall Flower Show. The show was being held on Saturday, and Mrs. Baxter was planning to enter her giant, double-blooming, rust and gold chrysanthemums. She was going to put them in a pewter vase and set the vase on the tea cloth which she had embroidered especially for the occasion.

This display, according to her, was sure to win. Everyone knew her chrysanthemums were outstanding. The tea cloth was all that was needed to tip the scales in her favor.

"And now, it's gone," she said, her voice quavering. "What, oh what, am I going to do?"

I couldn't help feeling sorry for Mrs. Baxter. She's a nice lady, and she's also sort of downtrodden. Not liberated at all, if you know what I mean. She's always cooking and cleaning for Tommy and Mr. Baxter. But she certainly does have a green thumb and, as far as I could tell, she really deserved to win that contest.

I looked at P. J. I could see she was thinking the same thing. "Don't worry, Mrs. Baxter," she said kindly. "We'll get it back for you."

Mrs. Baxter tried to smile. "It's nice of you to be so concerned," she said. "But I don't know. I just don't know."

Neither did the police officer.

He tried to sound confident, of course. He said there had been some reports of a prowler in the neighborhood. He asked if anyone had seen anything suspicious. (No one had.) And he had Mrs. Baxter check her laundry room just in case the wash was there. (It wasn't.)

Finally, he said that the Mill Creek police had a very good record for solving crimes, and that they'd probably have this one figured out in no time.

I have a feeling that was said for the benefit of Fred Scott, the newspaperman. He had been paying close attention and taking notes all the while. But from time to time an amused expression had flitted across his face.

I don't think it was caused by Mrs. Baxter and her

laundry or by the Mill Creek police, though. I think it was caused by us. By P. J. Clover and me.

Now, as the police officer wound things up, Mr. Scott turned to P. J. "You think you can solve this?" he asked.

"We're going to try," P. J. replied.

"How long do you expect it will take?" The reporter's voice was serious, but I could see that there was a twinkle in his eyes.

P. J. didn't seem to notice. Or if she did, she didn't care. "Not long," she said confidently. "Mrs. Baxter needs her tea cloth back by Saturday. We should have things wrapped up by then."

"By Saturday?"

"That's right."

Fred Scott made an effort not to smile. "May I quote you?" he asked.

P. J. beamed. "Why, of course," she said, lifting her chin a notch and smiling graciously (as if she were the Queen of England). "Of course you may." And just to make sure he had it right, she repeated herself. "We'll have things wrapped up by Saturday. By Saturday, or my name's not P. J. Clover, Private Eye!"

5
Clues

"P. J., are you crazy?" I hissed, after Fred Scott, the policeman, and the neighbors had finally left the yard.

"I don't think so," said P. J. innocently.

"Well, then how could you tell that reporter we'd have this case solved by Saturday? That's just two days away!"

"You're right, it is," P. J. admitted. Just for a second I thought I saw a shadow of doubt pass over her face. But it was gone—if it ever had been there—in a flash. "That's right, two days," she said briskly, brushing a strand of straggly blond hair out of her eyes. "We'd better get started right away."

And before I could make any more objections, she turned to Mrs. Baxter. "Do you mind if we have a look around?"

Mrs. Baxter started slightly, as if she'd forgotten we were there. "Oh, no, of course not," she replied absentmindedly.

Then, half to herself, she murmured, "Oh, why did this have to happen?" She ran a hand through her hair and gazed at the empty clothesline. "Five years. Five years in a row she's won and now she'll just do it again."

P. J.'s eyes lit up. "Who?" she asked. (I could tell she was trying not to sound too eager.)

"Who'll win again?"

Mrs. Baxter frowned. "Oh, no one. No one important," she replied quickly. Then, as if to change the subject, she glanced at her watch. "Why, it's nearly five o'clock," she said. "I've got to start dinner. And what's happened to Tommy? He should have been home long ago. Now where could he . . . ?"

But she was interrupted by the phone ringing inside the house. "Maybe that's him now," she said, heading for the back door. "Excuse me, girls."

The moment she was gone, I looked at P. J. and P. J. looked at me.

"A rival!" P. J. exclaimed. "She has a rival in this flower show. Someone she doesn't want to talk about. Someone who doesn't want *her* to win. Someone who doesn't want Mrs. Baxter's display to look as good as that gold-colored, embroidered tea cloth would make it look."

"But would someone steal, just to win a flower show?" I asked.

"I don't know," P. J. replied. "But we'll have to check it out. Meanwhile, let's have a look around here."

I flipped to a clean page in my notebook and followed P. J. through the back gate and into the alley.

The alley was the only way into and out of the Baxters' backyard. The Lee and Garrity houses, plus a vacant lot, were on one side (my own house was farther down), and P. J.'s house, the Baxters', and a neat white-frame house belonging to a retired school-teacher named Miss Pritchett were on the other.

I looked at Miss Pritchett's trim fence and her tidy trash cans. It seemed strange that *she* hadn't come running when Mrs. Baxter screamed. But maybe that was just as well. She was a fussy lady who seemed to have it in for every kid in the neighborhood. Knowing her, she'd probably have found some way of blaming the whole thing on *us*!

P. J. walked up and down, looking over fences and poking around trash cans. Most of the cans were open, the lids lying on the ground where the gar-bagemen—who usually collected the trash around one o'clock—had left them. The Baxters' and Miss Pritch-ett's, however, were neatly covered.

P. J. rapped her knuckles on the lid of the Baxters' can. "You know, there's something wrong here," she said slowly. "I can feel it, but I don't know exactly what it is."

I gazed first at the bushes behind the trash cans. (Could someone be hiding there?) Then, down at the ground.

In the dirt, just a short distance from P. J.'s feet, was a track!

"Look at this," I said, dropping to the ground beside the long, narrow, and very fresh-looking mark. "A bicycle track. Is that what you felt?"

P. J. looked excited. "I don't think so," she said,

"but this could be important. Look." She pointed to a hole gouged in the dirt a short distance from the track. "That must have been made by the kickstand. Someone must have parked a bike out here. And not too long ago, either."

A picture of the thief speeding away on a bicycle— the basket loaded with poor Mrs. Baxter's laundry— popped into my mind. I grabbed my pencil from behind my ear, where I'd tucked it for safekeeping, and quickly made a note in my book.

"Of course, we have to be careful," P. J. said slowly. "It might not mean anything. After all, anyone could leave a bike in the alley."

I wasn't used to seeing P. J. so cautious. But then, I wasn't used to seeing her as a private eye, either. I regarded her with new respect. Maybe in *this* venture she was going to look before she leaped. At least some of the time!

"We'd better check the backyard," she said, still businesslike. And with a final frown at the bicycle track and the Baxters' trash cans, she ducked back through the gate.

There seemed to be nothing in the yard that we hadn't already seen. Just an empty clothesline and the usual backyard stuff: a picnic table, some lawn furniture, the garden hose, and Mrs. Baxter's bed of double-blooming rust and gold chrysanthemums.

P. J. reached up and ran her fingers over the clothesline. She looked under the picnic table. She inspected the garden hose. When she got to the chrysanthemums, she looked first at the flowers and then at the earth which had been raked smooth along the edge of the bed.

Then, suddenly, she stopped.

"Now *this*," she said, kneeling down at the edge of the flower bed, "could mean something." She was looking at a footprint in the earth. "Did you notice Mrs. Baxter's shoes?" she asked.

I shook my head.

"Well, I did. They were low heeled with thick, rubber soles. She always wears shoes like that because she has trouble with her feet."

I looked at the print in the freshly raked earth. It was shaped like this:

And I saw what she meant.

"A woman!" I said. "A woman wearing high-heeled shoes has been standing in this flower bed."

I felt excitement creeping over me again. I opened my notebook and began to write. But then I stopped. If P. J. could be cautious, I could, too.

"This isn't anywhere near the clothesline," I pointed out. "It probably doesn't have anything to do with the laundry. Mrs. Baxter might have been showing her flowers to a friend or . . ."

But before I could say another word, P. J. grabbed my arm. Her hand felt cold. "Shhh," she whispered.

I stopped talking, and suddenly I heard a sound in the alley. There was a squeak and then a loud click—like a kickstand of a bike being set into place.

I looked at P. J. I remembered the tire track. I remembered that saying, the one about the criminal always returning to the scene of the crime.

Slowly, the gate from the alley opened.

My heart just about stopped.

Then . . .

"What are *you* doing here?!" demanded Tommy Baxter.

6

Trust No One

My feeling of relief at seeing Tommy (rather than some stranger who might be the thief) was mixed with surprise at the way he looked.

Usually, Tommy Baxter's a pretty clean sort of boy. Not spotless, of course, but *fairly* neat. Today, however, he looked like he'd been rolling in a pigpen.

His clothes were rumpled and muddy. The sleeve of his shirt was torn. His hair was mussed, he had smudges of dirt on his face, and what looked like the beginnings of a black eye.

I was about to ask what had happened, but P. J. didn't give me a chance.

Before I could say a word, she plucked a handful of leaves from Mrs. Baxter's chrysanthemum plants and stepped in front of Tommy, screening the footprint from view.

"We're taking some chrysanthemum cuttings," she said.

"We're doing what?!" I exclaimed.

31

But P. J. silenced me with a look that would have turned molten lava to ice.

Tommy's face seemed to have turned a shade paler beneath the dirt smudges.

"Leave those alone," he said. "They're my mother's. She's entering them in a flower show."

"I know, but she said we could have some," P. J. replied. "We're going to root them," she went on. (I noticed that the fingers of her left hand, which was hidden behind her back, were crossed.) Then, without skipping a beat, she added, "Did you have an accident?"

Tommy flushed.

"Fall off your bike?"

"No," he muttered.

"But you *were* riding your bike?"

(I was beginning to see what she was getting at. But it didn't make much sense. Not to me, at any rate.)

"Yeah, sure," Tommy replied. "It's out there." He waved his hand in the direction of the gate.

P. J.'s nose twitched slightly.

"Do you always park it in the alley?" she asked.

Tommy hesitated. "Sometimes," he said. "But what do you . . ."

"Did you park it there earlier this afternoon?"

P. J.'s question came quickly. So did Tommy's response. "Hey, what is this?" he said. (I don't think I'd ever heard him speak so sharply.) "The third degree? I don't have to tell you what I do. You've got your cuttings. Now why don't you just go home?" And with that, he stamped off across the yard and into his house.

"Touchy, touchy," murmured P. J., twirling the chrysanthemum leaves in her fingers.

"Wait until his mother sees him," I said as the Baxters' back door slammed shut. "He must have been in a fight."

"Looks like it," P. J. agreed.

That was strange, I thought. Tommy Baxter isn't the sort of boy who gets into fights. Not usually. He's not the sort of boy who storms away in a huff, either. It seemed odd all right. But then, a lot of peculiar things were going on.

"Do you think it was *his* bike that made that track?" I asked, remembering P. J.'s line of questioning.

"Could be," she replied.

"But that would mean he was here before," I said.

"That's right," she agreed again.

I looked at her in astonishment.

"Then why didn't you tell him what we're really doing?" I exclaimed. "Why go through all that stuff about taking chrysanthemum cuttings? I mean, Tommy might know something important. Why didn't you just ask if he'd been here?"

"Because," replied P. J. calmly, "I didn't want him to know that we're on the case."

"You didn't want him to know . . . But why not? He isn't a suspect. He wouldn't steal his own laundry, would he?"

P. J. shrugged. "I guess not," she admitted. "It

wouldn't make much sense. Still, we *do* have to remember one thing."

She moved closer to me. The late afternoon light was quickly fading, but I could see that her eyes were sparkling. "We have to remember," she said, "the first rule of the private eye . . . trust no one . . ." She glanced suspiciously around the shadowy yard, *". . . suspect everyone!"*

7
Butch

I have to admit I couldn't help breaking out in goosebumps, even though I knew she was being melodramatic. P. J. Clover has a way of making ordinary things seem *extra*ordinary. There we were in a plain, old backyard in plain, old Mill Creek and we might just as well have been in a murky London fog with Jack the Ripper on our trail. At least that's how I felt. And I can tell you, I was glad when I heard a familiar voice call, "P. J., P. J., I'm home!"

The spell was broken. It was Mrs. Clover. And if she was home from work, that meant it was half past five and my own mother would be starting to worry.

"Tomorrow," P. J. said as we parted. "In the clubhouse. After school. And remember . . . mum's the word!"

She meant that I wasn't supposed to tell anyone— at least not anyone who might be a suspect—that we were investigating the case.

Hah!

By the next morning, the whole world knew!

(Well, maybe not the *whole* world. Just everyone who lived in Mill Creek. Whi ..., believe me, was enough.)

And it was all P. J. Clover's doing.

This is the way it happened at my house.

I came down to breakfast. My father was buttering toast. My little brother, Victor, was munching crunchy granola. And my mother was reading the paper. *The Morning Gazette.* Fred Scott's column. All of a sudden, she gasped. "Stacy," she said, a look of astonishment on her face. "You're in the paper! You and P. J. Clover."

My father stopped buttering toast and leaned over my mother's shoulder as she began to read the last paragraph of Fred Scott's column out loud.

" 'The citizens of Mill Creek can rest easy knowing that an energetic police force is on the job. But just in case anyone should feel the need of further help, it's good to know that our town is blessed with two ambitious young private eyes. . . .' "

Victor stopped crunching his granola and leaned over my mother's other shoulder as she continued to read.

" 'P. J. Clover, together with her associate, Stacy Jones, . . .' "

"Wow," said Victor.

" '. . . were among the first to arrive at the scene of the crime in the Baxters' back . . .' "

"Oh, no!" I groaned. There went all hope of secrecy. And there also (now that I thought of it) came a new problem.

If my mother was reading Fred Scott's column in *The Morning Gazette*, might not the thief be reading it, too? A line from all of those old gangster movies I'd seen on TV suddenly came to me. You probably know the one. It always comes at the end, when one of the gang is about to get bumped off. "But why, why me?" the poor wretch cries. "Because you know too much," is the answer.

Did P. J. Clover and I know too much?

Of course, a pile of laundry didn't seem worth doing violence over. Still, you never could tell. There were all kinds of nuts around. I left my family chuckling over the column (Victor was actually hooting) and went to the phone to call P. J.

Mrs. Clover answered.

"Stacy," she said. "I was just about to call you. P. J.'s already left, but she asked me to give you a message. You're to go on to school without her. She'll meet you there. She said she had something important to do."

I wondered if it had something to do with the case. Or if maybe she was going down to *The Morning Gazette* to pop Fred Scott in the nose. "Has she seen the paper?" I asked.

P. J.'s mother sighed. "Yes, Stacy, we both have. And all I can say is I hope this doesn't turn out to be like that fortunetelling business. I don't want the phone ringing at all hours of the day and night again."

I could understand Mrs. Clover's concern. Still, I didn't think it was exactly fair of her to bring up the fortunetelling incident. (After all, who could have imagined that a few hundred advertising fliers handed out at the supermarket would bring such a response?) So, I said good-bye quickly and hurried to finish dressing for school.

I put on my most ordinary clothes. Nothing that would stand out. Nothing that would attract attention. Because after I'd thought about the thief knowing who we were, I'd thought of something else. The whole of Park School would probably know, too.

Unlike P. J. Clover, I do *not* like to be the center of attention. I'm more of an observer, I guess. Anyway, I was hoping that maybe if I looked as ordinary as possible no one would notice me. I was hoping that maybe—just maybe—no one from another class would say, "Hey, isn't that P. J. Clover's friend? Isn't that Stacy Jones? She was in the paper this morning. Associate private eye! What a joke!"

That was what I was hoping to avoid. But I didn't. Not at all. And again, it was all P. J. Clover's doing.

She was already at school when I got there. I didn't see her at first, though. The crowd was too big.

They were gathered on the tetherball court. Second graders, third graders, fourth graders. Even a few kindergarten kids were hanging around the outer edges, standing on their tiptoes, trying to figure out what was going on.

What *was* going on (I soon found out) was P. J. Clover holding court. That was what it looked like, anyhow.

There she was, tall and skinny as a scarecrow, blond hair as straggly as ever, standing in the center of the crowd. She was smiling and nodding (like the

Queen of England again) while everyone fired questions at her about what it was like to be interviewed by a reporter, and whether she really thought we'd solve the case by Saturday (Fred Scott had managed to get that in, too), etc., etc.

There was no chance of anyone—even if they were stupid or brand-new to the school—not knowing who she was. P. J. had seen to that by wearing her newest T-shirt.

My heart sank when I saw it. I had thought that shirt was pretty clever at first, but now it seemed downright dangerous. It came from Ireland. P. J.'s father—who's divorced from P. J.'s mother and who travels a lot—had sent it to her. It has a big green shamrock, which is a kind of Irish clover, on the front. P. J.'s dad had had her initials printed above. You can probably imagine what it looked like. But I'll show you just to make sure:

There. You see what I mean? Clever, but dangerous. Dangerous for someone who's supposed to be a *private* eye. Dangerous for someone on the trail of a thief. Dangerous for someone who might know too much.

It was also provoking, as P. J. soon found out.

I had just managed to worm my way through the crowd to her side.

When she saw me, her eyes lit up. "I've got something to tell you," she whispered. "Something important about . . ."

But before she could finish, there was a commotion at the edge of the crowd. Someone was shoving his way through. Someone with a freckled face, a tangle of curly brown hair, and a copy of *The Morning Gazette* in his hand. Butch Bigelow!

P. J. tensed. Butch was within two feet of her. Butch, her nemesis; Butch, the thorn in her side; Butch, the very one—though he didn't know it—who had launched her on her new career as a private eye!

As I said before, I don't think Butch is so bad. And seeing him there, standing in front of P. J., at least a head shorter and nowhere near as smart (in my opinion), my heart sort of went out to him. He'd seen the newspaper—that was clear—and it must have been too much for him. I expected him to at least try to come out with some smart comment, but he didn't. All he could manage was a lame, "Think you're pretty clever, don't you?"

P. J. relaxed, sort of like a cat who's caught a mouse and has decided to play with it. "More clever than some," she replied.

A few people in the crowd tittered.

If Butch had been smart, he would have left right then and there. But he isn't, so he didn't. He stayed. He shook the paper in P. J.'s face. "Some private eye," he said mockingly. "You don't know the first thing about crime. You can't solve this case in two days."

P. J. kept a smile on her face (I knew that was calculated to drive Butch crazy) and her voice calm. "Want to bet?" she said.

The crowd stirred and more people tittered.

Butch—poor guy—was taking the bait. His cheeks turned red. "You . . . you couldn't solve it in two *weeks*," he sputtered.

"Want to bet?" P. J. repeated calmly.

"You couldn't solve it in two *years*!"

"Want to bet?"

I wished she wouldn't keep saying that. I happened to know that Butch had twenty dollars which his famous aunt had sent him for his birthday. But *I* didn't have anything. And neither did P. J.

(Or so I thought.)

Butch—as it turned out—was doing some thinking, too. P. J. was making him look pretty foolish. And I could see that he was trying to think of something to come back with. Something that would turn the tables. Something that . . .

"Well, come on," P. J. prompted. "Do you want to bet or don't you?"

For a moment, Butch hesitated. Then, all at once, his face lit up. A gleam came into his eyes. He smiled.

I caught my breath. Something was going to happen. I could feel it. I could also feel that it was *not* something good. "Wait a minute," I interrupted. "Don't you think we should . . ."

But Butch paid no attention to me. He was looking at P. J. "O.K.," he said. "I'll bet. I'll bet you can't solve this case. I'll bet you can't solve it by Saturday like you told this reporter guy." He shook *The Morning Gazette* in P. J.'s face again. "I'll bet, but . . ." He paused and his eyes narrowed. "*I'll* set the terms."

P. J. was caught off guard. She opened her mouth as if she were about to speak. Then closed it again. I guess she hadn't really expected Butch to take up her challenge.

"Listen," I said quickly, seeing my chance. "Maybe betting isn't such a good idea. Maybe we should . . ."

"No," P. J. interrupted, recovering herself. She was not the kind of girl who could back down, even when it made good sense to do so. "I'm ready. Just name it," she said, holding out her hand. "Just name what you want to bet and we'll shake on it."

Butch's hand shot out like a rocket. Triumph was written all over his face. "All right," he said, pumping P. J.'s hand up and down. "But don't forget, you asked for it!"

"For what?" I said anxiously. The gleam in Butch's eyes was definitely a wicked one. "What do you want?"

"Nothing much," answered Butch, still gripping P. J.'s hand. "I'll put up my twenty dollars . . ."

Someone in the crowd gasped. Twenty dollars! That was big-time stuff.

"But we don't have . . ." I began.

"Don't worry," Butch said. "You don't have to put up a cent."

"But what . . ." I began again.

Butch held up his hand for silence. He looked at the crowd. He looked at P. J. He looked at me. And then he smiled. "All you have to put up," he said calmly, "is one thing . . . your clubhouse!"

8

"Don't Worry"

Any sympathy I'd felt for Butch Bigelow evaporated. I stared at P. J.'s hand clasped tightly in his. "You can't do it," I said. "Not the clubhouse. You can't bet that!"

"She already has," Butch pointed out. He gave P. J.'s hand a final shake and let it drop. "But don't worry, I'll take good care of it. I might even let you come and look at it. Sometime. Maybe." And with that, he smiled wickedly and strode away.

The first bell rang. The crowd of kids broke up.

"P. J.," I groaned. "P. J., this is awful!"

I expected her to agree.

But she didn't.

"Awful?" she said. "Stacy, it's terrific! The best thing that could have happened." Her eyes were sparkling. Her whole face was aglow with triumph and delight. "Didn't you see him? Didn't you hear him? Sounding off like that in front of that crowd of

44

kids. Why, by Monday, he'll be the laughingstock of the whole school! And we'll be twenty dollars richer. Just think of how we can fix up the headquarters with that!"

I couldn't believe what I was hearing. Butch, the laughingstock? Us, twenty dollars richer? "P. J.," I said angrily, "you're a little mixed up. It's you and me. *We'll* be the laughingstock. We walked right into his trap, and now we're going to lose our . . ."

But just then the tardy bell rang and there was no more time for talk. Our classroom was at the end of the main building and we had to run for it. As it was, we barely made it. We slipped through the doorway and into our desks just as the bell stopped ringing.

Butch Bigelow grinned when he saw us, but P. J. ignored him. She lifted the top of her desk and began to dig through the junk inside.

The classroom was quiet. I got out my math book and turned to the lesson for the day. My hands were shaking. But not from fear or excitement. No. They were shaking from anger. Anger at P. J. Clover. I glanced at her sitting there in her stupid T-shirt, a smug smile on her face. Who did she think she was? Betting our clubhouse, our beautiful clubhouse, just because she was too pigheaded to back down in front of Butch Bigelow.

I stared down at my math book. The numbers swam in front of my eyes. I swallowed hard. How could she do it? How *could* she?

"Hssst . . ."

I looked up.

It was P. J. Glancing cautiously in the direction of Mr. Collins, our teacher, she passed a folded-up piece of paper across the aisle to me.

I almost didn't take it. What could P. J. write that would make any difference now? But then, my curiosity got the better of me. I unfolded the note. P. J.'s scratchy handwriting jumped out at me. This is what it said:

9
The Grand Prize

Are you surprised?

Well, you couldn't be any more surprised than I was.

"What do you mean?" I whispered as soon as I read the note. "How could you . . ."

But Mr. Collins's warning voice interrupted me. "Remember, class, there will be no talking once the late bell has rung," he said, looking straight at me.

So that was the end of that.

We had a math test and a film called "The Wonderful Amazon" next, and then Melanie Cartwright gave one of her super-long reports ("Pollution: What It Means to YOU!"), so there was no time for any more whispering or writing notes.

It wasn't until the morning recess bell rang that P. J. and I finally had a chance to talk.

Not that it was easy.

Talking, I mean.

Because by this time even more people had heard

about the article in *The Morning Gazette*. What was more, they knew about the bet between P. J. and Butch and they were eagerly taking sides.

"Don't worry, P. J., you'll win," said some.

"Not a chance," said others.

Butch had installed himself on one of the benches outside the cafeteria and was sounding off to a circle of admirers. "Now, as my aunt says . . ." His voice carried clear across the schoolyard.

(If P. J. hadn't been busy smiling and nodding to her own fans, she probably would have walked right over and popped him in the nose!)

Meanwhile, all *I* wanted was to find out exactly what P. J.'s note had meant. I'd forgotten about being angry at her. I just wanted to know what was up. How could she know who had stolen Mrs. Baxter's laundry? All we had to go on was a bicycle track and a footprint. I didn't think even P. J. Clover could put those two things together and come up with the criminal's name.

Finally, five minutes before the recess ended, P. J. managed to break away from her fans. She grabbed me by the hand and pulled me toward the girls' lavatory. "I've got something to show you," she whispered as we ducked in the door.

There was no one inside, but for safety's sake, we went into one of the stalls and slid the bolt.

P. J. reached into the back pocket of her blue jeans and pulled out a crumpled piece of paper. "There," she said, holding it out triumphantly. "That's why I'm not worried about losing the clubhouse!"

I took the paper from her hand. It was an announcement. An announcement of the Mill Creek Garden Club's Fall Flower Show. It was torn at the top, as if it had been ripped from a bulletin board.

"That's what I was doing this morning," P. J. explained. "I remembered seeing this on the bulletin board at the Mill Creek Market. So I rode up there before school and sort of 'borrowed' it."

I started to read, but I wasn't quick enough for P. J. "The important part's at the bottom," she said, whisking the paper out of my hands (and almost dropping it into the toilet). "Listen to this: 'GRAND PRIZE: THE MOST OUTSTANDING FLORAL DISPLAY WILL BE AWARDED A GRAND PRIZE OF THE GARDEN CLUB TROPHY CUP, AND . . . $500!' "

"Five hundred dollars!" I grabbed the paper back to see for myself. "Wow! That's reason enough for Mrs. Baxter to care about winning!"

"*And* reason enough for someone else to want to stop her," P. J. said.

"You mean the rival?" I was beginning to see why P. J. was so sure of herself. "The one who's already won five years in a row?"

"Exactly!" said P. J. "And look here." She pointed to the last line of the announcement. FOR FURTHER INFORMATION CALL 381-2304. "As soon as school's over, we're going to call that number. We're going to ask for the name of the past winner. And when we get it, we'll have . . ."

"The name of the thief!" I finished for her.

P. J. beamed.

"Exactly!" she said.

10

Cover-Up

I could hardly wait for school to be over.

But P. J. didn't seem to be in any hurry. She had the Garden Club announcement tucked safely away in her pocket, that big green clover blazoned across her chest, and she was enjoying every last minute of her fame.

She smiled sweetly at Butch Bigelow whenever he looked in her direction, and she remained calm and unruffled when he described, at lunchtime, his plans for our clubhouse.

He was going to paint it black (ugh!) and hang a glow-in-the-dark skeleton left over from last Halloween on the door. He was also, he said, going to put up a sign—NO GIRLS ALLOWED.

That got him into an argument with Melanie Cartwright, who was already preparing her next report—"Women's Rights: An Idea Whose Time Has COME!"

It all made me very nervous.

Suppose P. J.'s plan didn't work? Suppose we

couldn't get the name of the past winner? Or if we did, suppose he (or she) wouldn't confess?

Something else was bothering me, too. Something more basic. This is what it was:

If someone had stolen Mrs. Baxter's laundry to ruin her chances of winning the Fall Flower Show, wouldn't he—or she—have to have known an awful lot? Wouldn't he have to have known, first, about the embroidered tea cloth; second, about its being in the wash; and third, about Mrs. Baxter being gone all afternoon?

"That's right," P. J. agreed when I told her.

(It was fifth period, P.E., which we always have with Mrs. Melton's sixth grade class. We were in the yard waiting to be chosen for dodgeball, so we could talk without getting into trouble.)

"But who could know all that?" I said.

"Anyone who wanted to," P. J. replied. "Mrs. Baxter wasn't keeping her chrysanthemums a secret. And she probably wasn't hiding the tea cloth, either. I'll bet she told everyone in the Garden Club about it."

That made sense.

Sort of.

"But I still don't see how the thief could have known that Mrs. Baxter washed the tea cloth and hung it on the line yesterday. Not to mention that she was going to be at her volunteer job all afternoon. Why, you'd practically have to live next door to know all that! And another thing," I went on before P. J. could interrupt. "If someone wanted to stop Mrs. Baxter from winning the flower show, why take *all* the laundry? Why not just take the tea cloth?"

At that, P. J. groaned and rolled her eyes in exasperation. "Where have you been, Stacy?" she said, putting her hands on my shoulders and giving me a shake. "Don't you go to the movies? Don't you listen to the news? Don't you know that when someone commits a *small* crime, they always go on to commit a *bigger* crime just to cover up?"

Again, what she said made sense. If someone wanted to steal the tea cloth, he might take all the laundry just to throw people—people like P. J. and me—off the trail. "Still, it seems like an awful lot for anyone to . . ." I began.

At the same time, a voice called, "Hey, I'll take the two ambitious young private eyes!"

I'd been so busy talking (and thinking) that I'd almost forgotten where we were. But now, the laughter of Mrs. Melton's sixth grade class brought me back.

I blushed (but P. J. smiled proudly) as we hurried to join the team we'd been chosen for.

A mixture of fifth and sixth graders was waiting for us. Melanie Cartwright was there and so was Tommy Baxter. His eye was really black now, and I was not surprised that he scowled at P. J. and me.

You could hardly blame him. He certainly knew by now that we hadn't been taking chrysanthemum cuttings in his backyard, and he was probably angry. No one likes to be tricked.

But I *was* surprised to see him standing beside Kurt Hoffman. Because Kurt was the one who'd given him that black eye. At least, that's what everyone was saying.

Tommy and Kurt (who's a big kid and a bully) had had a fight yesterday on the way home from school. (Something about the touch football team they both play on.) Kurt had won, I guess (after all, *he* didn't have a black eye), but now it looked like they'd made up.

As we took our positions for the game, Kurt leaned over and whispered something into Tommy's ear. Tommy didn't say anything. He just looked glummer than ever.

Then, for some reason, Kurt looked at me.

(P. J. was on the opposite side of the dodgeball area talking to Melanie. She didn't notice when Kurt stalked over to my side.)

I moved, thinking he wanted my place or something. But he didn't. He wanted me.

"Guess you and old hay-head over there"—he jerked his thumb in P. J.'s direction—"think you're pretty smart."

"Smart?" I echoed. "Why . . . uh . . . no."

I wasn't P. J. *I* wasn't about to challenge someone like Kurt Hoffman. (Kurt Hoffman, who took candy bars from kindergartners and filed his fingernails to ten sharp points . . . the better to scratch you with.)

"Well, you better *get* smart, then," he growled, glowering down at me. "Smart enough to forget this private-eye stuff."

"Huh?" I felt my mouth drop open.

It wasn't a very bright way to look.

It wasn't a very bright thing to say. But it was all that came to mind. If Kurt Hoffman had offered to buy me a banana split, I couldn't have been more surprised. Why should he care if P. J. Clover and I were private eyes? What was it to him?

But there was no time for explanations (not that Kurt would have given any!), because just then Mrs. Melton blew her whistle and the game began. Kurt managed to get in a parting shot, though.

"If you girls know what's good for you," he snarled as he started to move away, "you'll take my advice. Stick to a game you know how to play."

"And what's that?" I surprised myself by asking.

"Dolls!" he snorted.

11

A Phone Call

Dolls!

P. J. Clover and I hadn't played with dolls for years!

(Well, not *really* played with them.)

Who did Kurt Hoffman think he was, anyway?

"He's just jealous," P. J. said when I told her. "Probably wishes he was in the newspaper, too. But don't let it bother you. We've got more important things to do."

She patted the back pocket of her blue jeans and smiled significantly. "As soon as we make this phone call, we'll *really* get started!" she said.

That made me forget about Kurt Hoffman. It made me forget about everything, in fact, until we were out of school and back in the clubhouse.

"Let's call from here," I said.

P. J. agreed. "You open the window. I'll get the phone." She dashed across the yard and into her house.

The phone (I'd better explain here) is another special feature of our clubhouse (and another reason why we couldn't—we just couldn't—let it be lost to Butch Bigelow).

It works like this:

P. J. and her mom have an extra-long cord on their telephone. All we have to do is pass the phone out the bathroom window, across the yard, and through the clubhouse window, and presto! Our own private line. Butch, with all his plans for black paint and glow-in-the-dark skeletons, would never be able to come up with anything so ingenious as that!

In a moment, P. J. returned with the phone in one hand and a plate of sandwiches her mother had left in the refrigerator in the other. She passed both through the open window.

I put the phone on the table and picked up a peanut butter sandwich. P. J. came through the door, grabbed a banana-and-ketchup (one of her favorite combinations), and dug the wrinkled Garden Club announcement out of her pocket.

"Well, here goes," she said, swallowing a bite of (ugh!) sandwich and beginning to dial.

I could hear the phone on the other end ringing. Then a click and a faint, "Yes?"

Quickly, P. J. pinched her nose between her thumb and forefinger. "Hello, Garden Club?" she squeaked. "This is *The Morning Gazette* calling."

I almost choked on my sandwich.

Of course, it was a perfect way to get information. When P. J. explained that the paper was updating its files on the history of local clubs, the voice at the other end began to talk . . . and talk . . . and talk.

All P. J. could manage to squeeze in was an occasional "Yes ... uh-huh ... I see. ..." I was beginning to wonder if she'd ever be able to ask the crucial question, when suddenly, I heard her say, "What? What was that? Five years in a row, you say?"

My ears perked up.

"Who?" P. J. squeaked through her pinched nose. "Will you repeat that name? Oh! Well ... uh ... good-bye." She hung up the receiver abruptly and turned to me, her eyes wide with astonishment. "You were right," she said. "You were absolutely right!"

"I was?"

"Yes." She began to pace back and forth. "And it makes sense. It adds up. But it's not going to be easy."

"What are you talking about? How was I right?" I said. "*When* was I right?"

"In school," P. J. replied. "Remember you said that for anyone to know all those things about Mrs. Baxter and her laundry, they'd practically have to live next door?"

"Yes."

"Well ..." P. J. drew a deep breath. "That's just it. That's where the past winner of the Fall Flower Show does live!"

"But ... but *you* live next door to the Baxters," I said.

"On *one* side," P. J. corrected. "But on the other ..."

"You mean ..." My thoughts raced back to the day before. The neat, white-frame house, the picket fence, the tidy trash cans in the alley. And the question that had come immediately to mind. Why hadn't *she* come running like the other neighbors when Mrs. Baxter screamed?

"Miss Pritchett?" I said in amazement.

"Exactly!" P. J. replied.

12
Tommy

It was hard to believe. Though, as P. J. said, everything *did* add up.

Miss Pritchett *did* live next door to the Baxters. She *would* know that Mrs. Baxter worked on Thursday afternoons. And she *could* have sneaked into the Baxters' backyard.

Still, I just couldn't picture it.

I couldn't picture Miss Pritchett—finicky, neat, proper Miss Pritchett, who was always yelling at us kids to keep off her lawn and threatening to call the police if a ball came anywhere near her carefully tended flowers—creeping into the Baxters' backyard and making off with a load of laundry.

"Stranger things have happened," P. J. said. "When you're a private eye, you have to be ready for anything!"

"But what if we're wrong? We can't accuse someone of committing a crime without proof, can we?"

P. J. stopped pacing. "I guess you're right," she

said, a look of disappointment on her face. *She* had been all ready to charge right over there, an accusing finger pointing in Miss Pritchett's direction.

"Maybe we should go talk to her," I suggested, though I couldn't think of anyone I wanted to talk to less.

P. J. brightened. "Right," she agreed. "We'll ask a few key questions. *Then*, after we've got some evidence, we'll call the police.

The police! She said it as if she chatted with them every day. A picture of Miss Pritchett being led out of her house in handcuffs while the whole neighborhood watched came into my mind. It wasn't a fate I would wish on anyone!

"Maybe we won't have to call the police," I said. "Maybe she'll just give the tea cloth back and then everything will be all right."

"Maybe," P. J. said. "And maybe not. What we've got to do now, though, is find some excuse for talking to her. Something that won't arouse her suspicions. Something that . . ."

But just then, there was a loud knock on our clubhouse door. "Anyone in there?" a voice called.

I reached for the door handle. Then I remembered the eye. (There was no point in having a security system if you didn't use it!) Quickly, I swiveled the piece of black cardboard to one side and put my eye to the hole.

To my surprise, Tommy Baxter was standing outside. "Stacy?" he said, when he saw my eye peering out through the peephole. "P. J.? Is that you in there?"

I swiveled the cardboard back over the peephole and opened the door.

Tommy looked uncomfortable. "Can . . . can I talk to you?" he said.

P. J. and I exchanged a puzzled glance. "We're pretty busy," she said grandly. "But sure, come on in."

Tommy stepped through the doorway. He had a football tucked under his arm. His black eye had turned a mottled sort of brown. He surveyed the inside of the clubhouse. I could see that he was impressed, but he didn't say anything. In fact, seeing the inside of the clubhouse seemed to make him more uncomfortable than ever.

"On your way to practice?" I said, just to make conversation and maybe put him at his ease. "You're playing in the game Saturday, aren't you?"

Tommy's face turned red. "No," he said quickly. "I can't. Don't have a uniform. It was in the . . . the laundry."

The laundry? But of course. Now I remembered. Item six on the list of what was hanging on Mrs. Baxter's clothesline. Tommy's uniform. "Gee, that's too bad," I said. "You're the quarterback." (Tommy wasn't especially strong, but he was fast and that's what counts in a quarterback.) "Don't they have any extra uniforms?"

Tommy's face turned even redder. "No," he said quickly. "They don't. I mean they did, but now the coach can't find them. It doesn't matter, though. Kurt's taking my place."

"Kurt?" I echoed. I was thinking that I sure

wouldn't want to be on the opposing team with Kurt Hoffman in the lineup.

"Yeah," Tommy said, with an expression that was somewhere between a grin and a grimace. "Good old Kurt. And I'm carrying the football around because of my good old dad. He expects me to have it ready to toss the minute he comes home. He expects . . ." His voice had risen and it had an angry edge to it. "He expects . . ." But suddenly, as if he had remembered where he was, he stopped. He looked embarrassed.

P. J. stared at him.

And now *I* was embarrassed. P. J. doesn't always think about other people's feelings, but *I* do. I knew that Tommy had told us more than he meant to. More about himself and his dad, that is. And when someone does that, you shouldn't stare at them as if they were a fly under a microscope.

"Yeah . . . well . . . who cares about football, anyway?" I said quickly. "What did you want to talk to us about?"

"Yes." P. J. roused herself. "We don't have much time. We're on a case, you know," she said importantly.

Tommy turned a shade paler. "I know," he said. "That's what I wanted to talk to you about. I heard about the bet. And I'm sorry. I mean . . . I mean it sure would be a shame to lose this place." His words sort of tumbled out. "I know Butch. He's not a bad kid. Maybe if I talked to him, he'd be willing to forget it, or . . ."

"Butch? Forget it?" P. J. hooted. "No way. But don't worry. He's not going to win."

62

"What do you mean? You can't find the laundry," Tommy said. "The police can't even find it, so how can you . . ."

But P. J. wasn't listening. As Tommy was speaking, her eyes had fallen on the football he held under his arm. Her nose had begun to twitch as she looked at the brown leather. Then, suddenly, she pounced on it. "Tommy," she said excitedly. "Tommy, can we borrow this?"

"Huh?" Tommy looked surprised.

"Just for a minute," P. J. said, extracting the ball from him. "You'll get it right back. I promise." Her eyes were sparkling. "This is it, Stacy," she said, turning to me. "Exactly what we need. Come on!"

I didn't know what she was talking about. But there wasn't much I could do but follow her out the clubhouse door. She had the football in one hand and me in the other. She practically dragged me down the cement-block steps.

"Where are you going?" Tommy called.

"To tie things up," P. J. shouted over her shoulder. In the same breath she added, "Don't worry, this case will be solved in no time!"

13

Miss Pritchett

I didn't know what to think. My mind was still on Tommy and his dad and Butch and the clubhouse. And here was P. J., dragging me across her yard, through the hedge, and into the Baxters' backyard.

"Ready?" she said breathlessly.

Ready? "For what?" I gasped. But P. J. didn't stop to explain. She let go of my arm and rocked back on her heel. Her right arm—the arm with the football—swung back. With a mighty effort she heaved it (the football) into the air.

"P. J. !" I cried. "What are you doing? It's going to go right into . . ."

But before I could finish, the football had completed its journey up into the air over the Baxters' yard, up, up and over the white picket fence and then down—smack in the middle of Miss Pritchett's backyard.

"Are you crazy?" I said to P. J. "What did you want to do that for? Where does that get us?"

"It gets us to Miss Pritchett's front door," P. J. replied, heading around the side of the Baxters' house. "Don't you see? It's like I said. Exactly what we need. An excuse to go over there. An excuse to investigate!"

"But . . ."

But P. J. didn't stop. She came out on the Baxters' driveway, cut across Miss Pritchett's lawn, and bounded up the front steps with me hot on her heels. She had just raised her hand to knock when the door flew open.

Miss Pritchett glared down at us. She looked like the witch in *The Wizard of Oz*, except that her hair was tinted lavender. "Young lady," she said angrily, "What do you mean by walking across my lawn? Don't deny it. I saw you from the window. You went straight across my dichondra."

P. J. opened her eyes wide.

(I recognized it as her innocent look. She used it in class when she hadn't done her homework, or when she'd accidentally glanced at someone else's test paper.)

"Oh, I'm so sorry," she said, bowing her head humbly.

"Well, at least you have the decency to apologize." Miss Pritchett softened somewhat. "Not many young people would do that these days."

P. J., meanwhile, was taking a good, hard look at Miss Pritchett's shoes. They were high-heeled, and even without measuring them, I could see they were just the right size to have made that footprint in Mrs. Baxter's chrysanthemum bed.

I noticed that P. J.'s nose twitched slightly as she raised her head again.

"Well, what is it?" Miss Pritchett asked impatiently. "I'm a busy woman. I haven't got all day."

P. J. smiled sweetly. "Oh, I know," she said. "It must be a lot of work, keeping this house in such good shape and all. You probably never get a chance to go out."

"Well, I . . ." Miss Pritchett looked confused.

"Yesterday, for instance," P. J. went on quickly. "I'll bet you were here all day gardening and cleaning and stuff."

"As a matter of fact, I was," Miss Pritchett replied. "In the morning I trimmed my hedges and in the afternoon I waxed my linoleum and shampooed my rugs and then . . ." She hesitated. "But why am I telling you this?" she said abruptly. "What business is it of yours?"

"Oh, none, none at all," P. J. replied.

(I could tell she was having trouble keeping her voice—and her nose—steady.)

"I'm just interested in . . . in things," she explained vaguely. "The real reason I'm here is my friend's football. He lost it. In your backyard."

"In my backyard!" Miss Pritchett exclaimed. "How many times do I have to tell you children not to play your games around my house? I will not have you ruining my lawn and my flowers!"

"Oh, we wouldn't want to do that," P. J. said sincerely. "Especially not your flowers. You're entering a display in the Garden Club's Fall Flower Show, aren't you?"

At the words "Flower Show," Miss Pritchett seemed to forget her irritation. "Why, yes, I am," she replied proudly. Her chin went up a notch. "I've won the grand prize five years in a row."

"Five years," P. J. repeated, as if this were the first time she'd heard of it. "Imagine that! But I hear there's some pretty stiff competition this year."

Miss Pritchett flushed. "Oh, really?" she said.

"Yes," P. J. went on, smiling innocently. "Your neighbor, Mrs. Baxter, has quite a display planned. Just the other day, she was telling us about a special embroidered tea cloth . . ." She paused.

Miss Pritchett turned a shade darker when she heard Mrs. Baxter's name, but her expression didn't seem to change at the mention of the tea cloth.

P. J. frowned. She had obviously been expecting some sort of reaction, but when it didn't come, she went on (smiling again). "It will look lovely with her rust and gold chrysanthemums. You've seen *them*, I'm sure."

This time she got what she wanted.

Miss Pritchett turned red. A guilty expression flitted across her face. "No!" she snapped. "No, I haven't. Now go get your football and leave me alone!"

And with that, she shut the door in our faces!

14

The Eye Again

P. J. looked at me triumphantly.

"Well, what do you think of *that*?" she said. "Is she guilty or is she not?"

I had to admit that it didn't look good for Miss Pritchett.

She *had* been home yesterday afternoon. She had *not* come running when Mrs. Baxter discovered her laundry missing. And she had certainly *looked* guilty when P. J. mentioned the chrysanthemums.

Still, I couldn't shake a nagging doubt from my mind. Just being home when the crime was committed didn't prove anything. And as for the scream, well ... if Miss Pritchett was using a shampooing machine on her rugs, she might not have heard it.

Something else was bothering me, too. Tommy Baxter. Or rather, Tommy and Kurt.

I thought about it as P. J. ducked into Miss Pritchett's backyard to retrieve the football.

What had Tommy said? That he wasn't playing quarterback in the game Saturday, but Kurt was.

And what had Kurt said? At school, I mean. When he stalked across the dodgeball area. When he sneered down at me. *"You'd better get smart, then."* (That was it.) *"Smart enough to forget about this private-eye stuff. Stick to a game you know how to play. Dolls!"*

It meant something. I was sure of it. Otherwise, why would Kurt have bothered with me? But what? I couldn't quite put it all together.

"Listen, P. J.," I said when she returned with the football. "I think we've got to check out a few more things before we call the police."

(We were heading back to P. J.'s yard. Back to the clubhouse.)

"When Kurt said that stuff to me he must have . . ." I began.

But suddenly, P. J. interrupted me. "Stacy!" she exclaimed.

We were just rounding the corner of the Clovers' garage. I stopped and looked at her in surprise. Her eyes were wide and the freckles on her face stood out darkly.

"P. J.," I said, "what . . ."

"Look!" she breathed, pointing across the yard in the direction of the clubhouse. *"Look at the eye!"*

15

The Message

The knife was sticking straight out of the center of the eye.

It had been plunged in just above the peephole, at the point where the iris and the pupil met.

A piece of paper was held by the blade.

"It's some kind of a note," P. J. said, dropping Tommy's football and running toward the clubhouse.

I could feel my heart beating against my chest as I ran after her. My hands were like ice. And as I read the message, a cold shiver ran down my spine. It was made out of words and letters which had been cut from a magazine and glued into place. This is what it said:

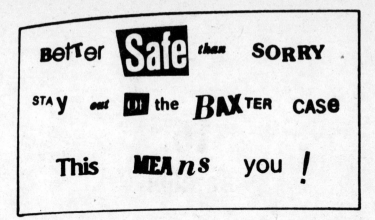

For a moment, all we could do was stare. It was the kind of note you read about in the newspapers. The kind kidnappers and murderers and mad bombers send. I felt cold all over, even though it was a warm afternoon.

Then suddenly, P. J. snapped her fingers. She turned to me, her eyes blazing, not with fear but with anger. "I know who did this!" she exclaimed.

She grabbed the knife and the note from the door. "This is a Boy Scout jackknife," she said. "Butch Bigelow is a Boy Scout. A Boy Scout who doesn't want to lose twenty bucks! He's trying to scare us off this case. That's what he's trying to do."

My fear turned quickly to anger.

"What a sneaky maneuver," I said. "And all so he can get his hands on our clubhouse and paint it black!"

P. J. looked at the glued-together message. " 'Better safe than sorry,' " she read disdainfully. "*He's* the one who's going to be sorry! Come on!"

16

An Alibi

Butch Bigelow's house was two blocks away and we covered the distance in record time. P. J. was still fuming as she knocked on the front door.

"Thinks he can scare us, does he," she muttered. "Well, we'll show him!"

The door opened.

As it did, a terrible sound hit my ears. I saw P. J. grimace. Mrs. Bigelow, who had opened the door, was grimacing, too.

"Why, hello, girls," she said weakly.

The sound seemed to grow louder. It was like cats fighting, dentists drilling, and fingernails being scraped against a blackboard all at the same time.

"Is Butch here?" P. J. managed to ask.

Mrs. Bigelow sighed. "Oh, yes, he's here," she said. "Come in."

She stood aside so we could enter. "Butch! Butch!" she called. "You can stop now. You've got company."

With a final screech, the awful noise ended and Butch appeared from the next room. He was holding a violin and bow in one hand.

When he saw P. J., his face turned red. He dropped the instrument on the nearest chair and moved in front as if to hide it from view. "What do *you* want?" he said.

P. J. looked at the half-concealed violin in amazement. "I didn't know you . . ." she began.

"Well, I do," Butch interrupted. "Want to make something of it?"

"Butch, that's no way to talk to guests," Mrs. Bigelow warned. "Now ask your friends to sit down. I'll go make some lemonade." She hurried off in the direction of the kitchen.

Butch's face turned red again.

I felt a little sorry for him (even though he had stuck the note on our clubhouse door). No one likes to be talked to like that by his mother.

P. J. must have felt a twinge of sympathy, too, because she dropped the violin stuff and went straight to the main point.

"You know why we're here," she said.

Butch's face looked blank.

P. J. held the note and jackknife out to him. "No use denying it," she said. "Who else would pull a stunt like this?"

Butch took the note. His eyes opened wide as he read it.

"Better take the knife, too," P. J. said. "It's yours."

"Oh, no, it's not." Butch fished around in the back

pocket of his blue jeans. "This is mine." He pulled out a battered Boy Scout knife. "And if you think I wrote this note, you're wrong there, too."

"Oh, yeah? Then tell us where you were for the last half hour."

Butch looked at the violin. He didn't have to say anything. He had an alibi, all right. A screechy one, but an alibi all the same.

For once, P. J. was at a loss for words.

And who could blame her? If Butch hadn't stuck the note on our door, who had? Certainly not Miss Pritchett. No matter how guilty she seemed, there was no way she could have slipped into P. J.'s backyard with the note. We had been with her the whole time. But if she didn't, who did?

Butch seemed as interested as we were. He looked at the note again. "You know, I bet I could figure out who put this together," he said slowly. "All you have to do is find out what newspapers and magazines these words came from and then . . ."

"And then find out who subscribes to them," P. J. interrupted, recovering herself. She leaned over Butch's shoulder to study the note. "That wouldn't be too hard," she said, her voice beginning to sound excited.

(She seemed to have forgotten who Butch was. Her nemesis, her enemy, the boy who was planning to paint our clubhouse black!)

"Look, you can tell this comes from *The Morning Gazette*."

"And this is from *Boy's Life*," Butch put in, pointing to a capital *B*.

74

"And I'll bet this is from *Woman's Day*, and . . ."

"Now that's what I like to see!"

Butch and P. J. both looked up from the note as Mrs. Bigelow came back into the room, a tray of lemonade glasses in her hands.

"Young people working on a project together," she said. "Cooperation, mutual aid . . ."

(Mrs. Bigelow was a social worker and tended to talk like that.)

". . . the spirit of friendship."

Butch dropped the note like a hot potato.

P. J. caught it.

They stared at each other. P. J.'s eyes narrowed. Butch's did, too.

I figured I'd better step in . . . fast.

"Thanks for the lemonade," I said to Mrs. Bigelow. I grabbed P. J. by the arm and pulled her toward the door. "But I'm afraid we have to go."

Butch pulled himself together. "Yeah, you've got a lot of work to do." He grinned wickedly, looking like his old self again. "But if I were you, I wouldn't bother. It'll take days to trace down that note. Face it, you can't win, Clover!"

"Butch . . ." P. J. growled. "You'd better . . ."

I dragged her out the door.

"I'll be over in the morning," Butch called after us.

"What for?" P. J. shouted.

"To measure."

"Measure what?"

"My clubhouse," Butch crowed. "I want to be sure to buy enough paint!"

75

17
Red Herrings

I wasn't used to seeing P. J. Clover discouraged. It didn't happen often. But it was happening now.

She opened her mouth as if to shout something back, then closed it again.

The Bigelows' door slammed shut with a bang.

"What a creep!" I said, as we headed back to the sidewalk. "Measuring our clubhouse. Who does he think he is?"

"The new owner," replied P. J. dismally.

My heart sank.

Was P. J. giving up?

Was her brilliant mind failing?

"Maybe you need a sandwich," I said, as we turned into the Clovers' backyard. "Pickle and peanut butter. I'll make it for you. It'll help you think."

But P. J. waved my offer away.

"No," she said, a serious expression on her face. "No time. We've got to concentrate. Review the evidence. Check the clues." She headed for the clubhouse, motioning for me to follow.

I was glad to see that her spirits were improving, but I wasn't sure about mine.

I looked at the eye. There was a rip in the paper where the knife had been stuck. I shivered. Being angry at Butch had made me forget how I'd felt when I first saw the knife in the eye. But now, it all came back. The gleaming blade, the ugly words. It wasn't a joke. And now we knew it hadn't been Butch Bigelow who put the message there.

(And it certainly hadn't been Miss Pritchett!)

It was someone else. Someone who was serious about scaring us off the case. I thought of the phone sitting on the clubhouse table. P. J. might have her mind on reviewing the evidence and checking the clues, but I had a better idea. The police. If this wasn't the right time to call them, I didn't know what was.

"P. J.," I said, following her into the clubhouse. "Don't you think we'd better . . ."

But P. J. didn't give me a chance to finish. She was pacing back and forth, no longer looking discouraged. "Stacy," she said when she saw me. "I think I've got it!"

"You mean you know who stuck the note on our door?"

"Not yet. But I see where we went wrong. We've been chasing a red herring!"

"A what?"

"A red herring," P. J. repeated. "In mystery

books—the kind Butch's aunt writes—the trail always leads to someone who *could* have committed the crime, but didn't. That's called a red herring. And that's what Miss Pritchett is. But the thief is someone else!"

"Yeah, someone dangerous," I said. "Listen, I think the police ..."

But P. J. wasn't about to stop.

"Our problem is we've been thinking wrong," she went on, pacing back and forth across the clubhouse floor. "Just because Mrs. Baxter mentioned her rival, we've been thinking that's who it was. But maybe it's someone else. After all, the prize in that flower show is five hundred dollars. Anyone would want to win that."

"Or maybe ..." I hesitated. Because, as P. J. was speaking, the thoughts I'd been having before we found the note on the door floated back into my mind. What was it that Tommy Baxter had said? That he wasn't playing in the touch football game because his uniform had been in the stolen laundry. That the coach couldn't find the extra uniforms. And that Kurt ...

"P. J.!" I said. "Wait a minute. Maybe we're *really* on the wrong track. Maybe it's not Miss Pritchett that's the ... the ... the fish ..."

"You mean the red herring," P. J. corrected.

"Herring, sardine, who cares!" I could feel my excitement mounting. I was onto something. I knew it. "Hand me my binder," I commanded P. J.

She looked surprised, but she picked up my school

binder from the chair where I'd dropped it and passed it to me.

It was there. At the back, behind my social studies papers, neatly copied out from the notes I'd taken the day before. Mrs. Baxter's laundry list.

I held it out to P. J. "There's your herring," I said, pointing to item number eight—*Gold-colored tea cloth embroidered with chrysanthemums.*

"Huh?" For once, P. J. looked baffled.

"Don't you see?" I said. "We've been looking for the wrong thing. We've been thinking the laundry was stolen because someone wanted to get that tea cloth and keep Mrs. Baxter from winning the prize. But there's more than one competition going on this Saturday."

I ran my finger up the list to item number six— *Football uniform (Tommy).* I looked at P. J. A light was beginning to dawn in her eyes.

"You mean, the football game," she said in a hushed voice. "The football game that's taking place this Saturday. The game that Tommy can't play in because his uniform's gone . . ."

I could practically hear the gears in her mind start shifting. Her nose was beginning to twitch. "Stacy, you're right. Tommy's a good player. Even if he doesn't love the game, he's fast. If the other team— the team they're going to play tomorrow—could get rid of him, they'd . . ."

But she was wrong.

I was sure of it.

"No," I said. "It's not the other team. It's worse

than that." The scene on the dodgeball area flashed into my mind. "It's someone on his own team. Someone who'll get to play quarterback if Tommy can't. Someone . . ." I paused to let what I was about to say sink in. "Someone who already gave Tommy Baxter a black eye."

"You mean . . ."

I nodded. "That's right," I said. (And now I was sure of it. *Absolutely* sure.) "It's got to be. It can't be anyone else. It's Kurt. Kurt Hoffman!"

18

Exactly Twenty-Four Hours

Now was the time to call the police. The phone was ready and waiting on the table. I reached for the receiver.

"What are you doing?" P. J. said.

"Calling the police," I replied.

"You can't do that," she said.

"Why not?" I looked at her in astonishment. "Stealing's a crime. The police should know about it. Besides, Kurt Hoffman could be dangerous. You saw how Tommy Baxter looked after that fight."

But P. J. shook her head. "We've got to handle this ourselves," she said. "Don't you see? That's the only way Butch won't win the bet. If we call the police now, he'll say we didn't really solve the case. He'll show up tomorrow with a can of black paint and his glow-in-the-dark skeleton!"

She had a point. It would be just like Butch to do that.

But confronting Kurt Hoffman and accusing him

of committing a crime ... Well, that was *not* something that *I* wanted to do.

"Don't worry," P. J. said confidently, all her old brashness back. "All we have to do is tell him what we know. When he realizes he's trapped, he'll confess. *Then* we'll say he can either give us the laundry or we'll call the police."

That *sounded* reasonable. Still, I wished that Kurt weren't so big. *And* so mean.

P. J. didn't seem to be bothered by any such thoughts. She stuffed the jackknife and the glued-together note into her back pocket. "Dilly's," she said. "That's where we'll find him. That's where he hangs out."

She grabbed my wrist and looked down at my watch. "Perfect!" she pronounced. "It's 3:45. Exactly twenty-four hours—one day—from the discovery of the crime and we've already gotten it solved. The clubhouse is still ours and ..." She paused and rubbed her hands together with glee. "And old Butch Bigelow's twenty dollars is in our pockets!"

19
Kurt

Dilly's Ice Cream Shoppe was everyone's favorite place.

That was all for the better (as P. J. pointed out), because there would be plenty of witnesses. Lots of kids from school, plus Mr. Dilly himself. A man whom everyone trusted.

"This is better than I ever thought it would be," P. J. said as we raced toward the shop. "Private eyes for just one day and we've already solved our first case. What a reputation we're going to have! We'll really be in business after this!"

I had to admit it sounded good. But unlike P. J., I knew I wouldn't feel like celebrating until I actually heard Kurt Hoffman confess.

(I hoped, too—now that I'd had time to think about it—that Kurt would just give the laundry back. Then everyone would be happy. Mrs. Baxter could enter the flower show, Tommy Baxter could play in the game, and Kurt wouldn't have to go to jail—or wherever they send sixth graders who take people's laundry. I didn't want to be responsible for anyone—not even a bully like Kurt Hoffman—wasting away in a jail cell!)

I was out of breath when we reached Dilly's.

The shop was crowded and noisy, as usual, and at first I thought that Kurt wasn't there.

But then I saw him.

He was in a rear booth, surrounded by his pals. He was eating a hot fudge sundae and between bites he was bragging. "Just wait till you see me out there on that field tomorrow," he said. His voice carried over the din in the shop. "Namath, Simpson, they won't have a thing on me!"

P. J. paused. Just for a second, I thought I saw something like doubt cross her face. Kurt *did* look big. And he *did* sound tough.

"We *could* call the . . ." I began.

But P. J. shook her head. "No, we've got to go through with this," she said. "It's the only way." And with that, she lifted her chin a notch, tugged her T-shirt (with the big clover on it) into place, and marched straight up to Kurt Hoffman's booth.

I followed, shaking in my sneakers.

Kurt looked surprised to see us. He broke off in the middle of a sentence. "Well, look who's here. The two ambitious young private eyes," he said snidely. "What do *you* want?"

"You," P. J. said.

"Huh?" Kurt frowned. "What are you talking about?"

"I think you know," P. J. replied.

(I wondered if her heart was pounding as hard as mine.)

"You're playing quarterback in the game tomorrow, aren't you?" she said.

"What if I am?" Kurt replied.

"You wouldn't be, if Tommy Baxter could."

Kurt flushed. "So what?" he said. "What difference does that make? Tommy can't play, I can. There's nothing wrong with that."

"There is if you're the reason why he can't play." P. J.'s voice was steady.

Kurt looked uneasy.

By this time a crowd had gathered around the booth. Even Mr. Dilly looked up from a banana split he was assembling to see what was going on.

"Everyone knows that you had a fight with Tommy," P. J. continued. Her voice sounded loud in the silence that had fallen over the shop. "And I'll bet it was about the game. I'll bet you tried to scare him into not playing so that you could be quarterback. Then, when that didn't work, you did something else."

Kurt's eyes narrowed. He looked around at the crowd of kids. "I didn't do anything," he muttered. "She's crazy."

"Oh, yeah?" P. J. said. "Then how do you explain this?" She pulled the glued-together note and the jackknife from her pocket and flung them on the table.

Everyone leaned forward as Kurt picked up the knife, looked at it, and then read the note. A hint of a smile played over his face. "Boy, he's really ..."

he murmured. Then, as if he suddenly remembered where he was, he stopped.

"Are you saying *I* had something to do with this?" he said.

I felt uneasy. Something was wrong. I didn't know what, but Kurt was not acting the way I had thought he would.

P. J., however, didn't seem to notice.

"Not only with that," she said, "but with Mrs. Baxter's laundry, too."

"So that's it!" Kurt leaned back in the booth and grinned wickedly. "Little Miss Know-It-All thinks she's got it all figured out."

"I don't think, I *know*," P. J. charged. "And it'll be easier for you if you just admit it. So come on. Out with it. Where were you on Thursday afternoon?"

Now, Kurt really smiled. A broad grin stretching from ear to ear spread over his face. "Where was I on Thursday afternoon?" he repeated. "Thursday afternoon when the famous Baxter laundry was stolen." He looked over at Mr. Dilly, who had just sprinkled a spoonful of nuts over the banana split. "Why don't *you* tell them?" he said.

I felt a sinking sensation in my stomach.

Mr. Dilly shrugged his shoulders apologetically. "He was here," he said.

"Here?" P. J. looked at Mr. Dilly in astonishment. "But he couldn't have been. He . . ."

"He was," Mr. Dilly said. "He ordered a Firehouse Special and then he couldn't pay, so I made him wash dishes."

I looked at the big metal sink behind the counter.

Then at Kurt, grinning triumphantly.

And then at P. J.

The clover on her shirt seemed to wilt.

"I wish I could help you," Mr. Dilly said. "But I've got to tell the truth. Kurt was here. Right here at that sink *all afternoon*."

20

The Tea Cloth

How we got home, I don't know.

Neither of us spoke.

(Not that I remember.)

But when we entered P. J.'s backyard, and when we saw our clubhouse (our beautiful clubhouse) with the eye on the door and the telephone cord through the window, we turned to each other.

P. J.'s eyes were sparkling. But this time it wasn't from excitement. "Oh, Stacy," she said. "I'm such a dope. I never should have made that bet. It was stupid. Stupid!"

"No, it wasn't," I said quickly.

(I couldn't stand seeing P. J. down on herself. It was wrong. All wrong. *I* was the one who worried, not her!)

"It looked like a sure thing," I went on. "It *was* a sure thing until dumb old Kurt . . ."

"Girls!"

A voice floated over the hedge separating the Baxters' yard from the Clovers'.

"P. J., Stacy. Come here quick. I have something to show you."

We turned to see Mrs. Baxter waving to us excitedly over the hedge.

P. J. perked up. "What is it?" she said as we hurried into the Baxters' yard.

"It's my tea cloth," Mrs. Baxter replied. "Look!"

I could hardly believe my eyes. It couldn't be. But there it was. Hooked to the clothesline by a couple of wooden pins, flapping merrily in the breeze for all the world to see, was a square of gold-colored fabric. Gold-colored fabric with a bright pattern of chrysanthemums embroidered around the edges. The tea cloth. Mrs. Baxter's stolen tea cloth!

21
Garbage!

"But how . . ." P. J. began.

"When?" I asked. "Who?"

Mrs. Baxter shook her head. "I don't know," she said. "All I know is that when I came home from the grocery a few minutes ago I looked out the kitchen window and there it was! As soon as I saw it, I ran out here and called you. I wanted you to see it for yourselves, just as I found it, because you know what? I think *you're* responsible for this!"

"Who, us?" I was too baffled to say anything brighter than that.

"Yes." Mrs. Baxter crossed to the clothesline and took down the cloth. "I think that whoever stole the laundry must have read that article in *The Morning Gazette*. They felt guilty when they learned how important this tea cloth is to me, and so they put it back!" She ran her hand fondly over the cloth. "It renews my faith in human kindness," she said. "That's what it does."

P. J., who had been standing dumbfounded through all this, suddenly roused herself. She looked hard at the cloth in Mrs. Baxter's hands.

I saw her nose begin to twitch.

"Could I see that?" she asked.

"Certainly," Mrs. Baxter said, handing her the cloth. "It's beautiful, isn't it? You can see why . . ."

"Was this clean?" P. J. interrupted.

(Her nose was really twitching now.)

"I mean when you put it on the line?"

"Why, of course," Mrs. Baxter replied. "I'd just washed it."

"Well then," P. J. said, holding the cloth up, "whoever stole it ate dinner on it, too!"

I stepped forward to inspect the cloth more closely. She was right. There were stains along one edge. Some orange and greasy, others a rich brown.

"Spaghetti," P. J. said. "Spaghetti and maybe chocolate pudding for dessert."

"Why, how strange," Mrs. Baxter murmured. "That's exactly what we had for dinner last night."

"You did?" P. J. had a funny look on her face. Thoughtful and excited at the same time.

"Yes. It's one of Tommy's favorite meals," Mrs. Baxter said. She smiled. "That boy's been so good since all this happened. He's been worried about my display for the flower show and brave about not being able to play in the game tomorrow. He hasn't even complained about the black eye he got in that silly fight. And thoughtful. Why, he's actually been taking out the garbage without being told!"

"The garbage?" P. J.'s voice had a strange note in it.

"Yes. I usually have to nag him, but since yesterday . . ."

"Oh, my gosh!"

P. J. grabbed my arm. Her face was lit up like a Christmas tree. "The garbage!" she exclaimed. "That's what was wrong. That's what I felt!"

"Huh?" I didn't know what she was talking about.

"In the alley," she said. "Yesterday. Don't you remember? Stacy! Mrs. Baxter! I know where it is. I know where the rest of the laundry is!"

22

Absolutely Brilliant

After that, everything happened very fast.

P. J. started running, dragging me with her, across the Baxters' backyard and through the gate to the alley.

Mrs. Baxter followed.

And Tommy Baxter suddenly appeared at the back door.

"Wait!" he cried.

But it was too late.

P. J. and I had reached the trash can. P. J.'s hand was already on the lid.

"Don't!" Tommy shouted.

But P. J. paid no attention. She pulled off the lid and let it drop to the ground with a clatter.

"Oh, my goodness!" Mrs. Baxter exclaimed.

"Oh, no," Tommy groaned. He was beside us by this time.

I tried to say something, but the words wouldn't come. All I could do was stare. There it was. Mounds of it. Whites, plaids, polka dots, pastels. The trash can was filled. Filled with laundry. And on top of it all was a brown paper bag. A patch of spaghetti sauce spread greasily from the bottom and a trickle of chocolate pudding oozed out the side, staining the clothes that it touched. Orange and brown. Just like the tea cloth.

"But how . . ." Mrs. Baxter began. "Who . . ."

"I think Tommy's the one who can tell you that," said P. J. quietly.

I won't try to put down everything that happened next. Tommy Baxter had a lot of explaining to do. And it took a while before Mrs. Baxter calmed down enough to listen.

"Now, let's get this straight," she said at last. "You had a fight after school with Kurt Hoffman because he wanted to play quarterback in the game this Saturday. So you came home, parked your bike in the alley, took the laundry, including your football uniform, off the line and hid it in the trash can . . . all so that you *couldn't* play?"

"I had to," Tommy said. "And I hid the extra uniforms, too, so the coach couldn't find them. It was the only way. I knew that Dad would never understand if I said I didn't want to be in the game. He would have told me to stand up to Kurt. But I couldn't do that. I couldn't because of what Kurt said he would do."

"Which was what?"

Tommy hesitated. Then, "Rip up your chrysanthemums," he muttered.

94

"Rip up my . . . oh . . ." Mrs. Baxter's voice, which had been edged with irritation, suddenly changed. "But that means . . . Why, Tommy, you did all this for me?"

Tommy flushed. "Well, not exactly," he murmured.

He looked at P. J. and me.

"Oh, what's the use," he sighed. "I might as well face it. I told myself I was taking it because of you, Mom. But I wasn't. I was doing it for myself. I don't want to play in that game tomorrow. I don't want to ever play in any football game. I hate it! I like drawing, painting, and stuff like that. But Dad . . . Well, he doesn't understand, so old Kurt just gave me an easy way out."

For a moment, no one said anything.

Then Tommy went on in a husky voice. "See, I didn't know about the tea cloth. I knew about the chrysanthemums. Everyone knows about your chrysanthemums, Mom, even Kurt. But I didn't know about the tea cloth. I just took all the laundry so it wouldn't look suspicious. Then I didn't know what to do. I didn't know what to do about the police, or about the tea cloth. And then I heard about the bet P. J. had made. I didn't want them to lose their clubhouse, but I couldn't have them finding the laundry before the game tomorrow. I *had* to get them off the trail . . ." His voice fell and he scuffed his shoe in the dirt.

"You *did* manage to scare us," I said.

"Well, I had to do something," Tommy murmured. "P. J. said she just about had it solved."

(P. J. and I exchanged a glance. But we didn't say a word. We could give Tommy his knife and his note back later on. There was no need for Mrs. Baxter to know *everything*.)

"I thought that if I got the tea cloth out of the trash and hung it on the line you'd think that the thief gave it back," Tommy went on. "Anyway, you'd have it for the flower show and maybe, if I talked to Butch, he'd agree to call the bet off."

Mrs. Baxter put her hand on Tommy's shoulder. "I can see you've had plenty to think about," she said quietly. "Maybe we're all going to have to do some more of that. Thinking, I mean. And talking. You, me, and your dad, together."

"But Dad . . ." Tommy began.

"Your father is who he is," Tommy's mother said. "You have to be who you are. I'm afraid we've lost sight of some important things in this family. We've got some catching up to do. But I know your father's proud of you. And not just because of football."

"Gee, Mom . . ." Tommy looked at his mother. Then at us. And then down at the laundry. He blinked hard a few times.

It was very quiet in the alley.

Then, P. J. cleared her throat loudly. "Well, isn't anyone going to ask?" she said.

"Ask?"

"About the laundry. About how I knew it was here."

"That's easy," I said. "It was the stains. Spaghetti and chocolate stains on the tea cloth."

"Yes," Mrs. Baxter agreed. "And my telling you

that Tommy was taking out the garbage without being told."

"Partly," P. J. said. "But it was remembering the way I'd felt when we were out here in the alley yesterday that really did it. Remember how it looked, Stacy?"

I gazed up and down the alley. It was different than yesterday. Different. But I wasn't sure why.

"It was the trash cans!" P. J. said triumphantly. "Yesterday when we came out here most of the cans were uncovered. The lids were lying on the ground where the garbage collectors had left them. *Except* for Miss Pritchett's and the Baxters'."

"But Miss Pritchett's so neat," I said. "She probably ran out and covered hers the minute the garbage collectors were through."

"Right," P. J. agreed. "I think she did one more thing, too. She knew Mrs. Baxter wasn't home and so she sneaked into the yard for a look at the chrysanthemums."

"Sort of sizing up the competition," I said. "P. J., I'll bet you're right. It would be just like her and it would explain that footprint."

"It would," P. J. said. "But how about the Baxters' garbage can? Miss Pritchett certainly wouldn't have bothered to cover that. And no one was home at the Baxters' house. So how did the cover get put back on? That's what was bothering me, though I couldn't quite put my finger on it. Then, when Mrs. Baxter mentioned the garbage, it all came together. I remembered the bicycle track and the touchy way Tommy had acted, and suddenly I saw it all!"

97

She smiled a smile of triumph and delight.

"It was brilliant," she said.

(I blushed at her immodesty.)

"Absolutely brilliant!"

I thought that the next thing P. J. would want to do was call Butch Bigelow.

That's what *I* wanted to do.

I wanted to go straight to the clubhouse (*our* clubhouse) and phone him (on *our* phone) and tell him he could forget about black paint and glow-in-the-dark skeletons and any other crazy things he might have in mind.

But P. J. had a better idea.

She made a phone call, all right.

But it was not to Butch.

"Just wait," she said as she hung up the phone. "Just wait until tomorrow morning. Just wait until you see it!"

"See what?" I said.

(I knew who she had called. But I did not know what she meant.)

"The look," P. J. replied triumphantly. "The look on poor old Butch Bigelow's face!"

23

A Present

I was at P. J.'s house bright and early.

Mrs. Clover greeted me. "Well, I guess you and P. J. have a new career," she said, with a sort of long-suffering smile. "She's out in the backyard making some last-minute adjustments to your new office."

P. J. grinned when she saw me. She was kneeling by the clubhouse door, a dripping paint brush in her hand. "Like it?" she asked.

I did!

"All it needs is a comma between Jones and associate," I said.

P. J. obliged and then stood back to admire her work.

It looked good. It looked *very* good.

"Will they be here soon?" I asked.

"Nine o'clock," P. J. replied.

I looked at my watch. "It's a quarter to nine now," I said. "But how about Butch? Do you think he'll show up? I mean, he could have changed his mind."

"No chance of that!" P. J. said.

And of course, she was right.

At five minutes to nine, Butch—equipped with a tape measure, paper, and pencil—appeared in the Clovers' backyard.

He looked at the clubhouse door.

(I could see he was impressed.)

"Clever," he admitted, nodding his head approvingly at the eye. "I'll have to tell my aunt about it. Maybe she can use it in one of her books. But too bad you went to all that trouble."

"Oh, I don't know," P. J. said offhandedly. "I think it was worth it. It'll look good in the pictures."

"Pictures?" Butch said. "What pictures?"

"For *The Morning Gazette*," P. J. replied. "You see, my associate and I . . ."

But before she could finish, Mrs. Clover called out the kitchen window, "P. J., the people from the paper are here."

"The paper? Hey, what's going on?" Butch exclaimed.

He stared as Fred Scott, followed by a woman with a camera, came out of the house.

"Congratulations," the reporter said, extending his hand first to P. J. and then to me. "I didn't think you could do it."

"Do what?" Butch squawked. "Will somebody tell me what's going on?"

The photographer arranged P. J. and me in front of the clubhouse.

Fred Scott turned to Butch. "Don't you know?" he said. "They've solved it. The case of the stolen laundry!"

The shutter snapped.

"Beautiful, girls," the photographer declared.

But I thought she had her camera pointed the wrong way.

She should have had it turned on Butch. If she had, she would have caught one of the strangest expressions ever seen. Shock, anger, envy, and yes . . . even admiration . . . all were mixed together on Butch's freckled face. "You mean you . . . you . . . solved it?" he sputtered. *"You?"*

"Who else?" replied P. J. coolly.

The photographer packed up her camera.

"Thanks for calling us," Fred Scott said. "Of course, since it turned out to be a family affair, I won't write it up in my column. But we can use the picture for a story we're doing. A story on enterprising youth. And here, I brought you a present."

He reached into the pocket of his sports jacket and pulled out a small box.

"I had the printer run these off before we went to press yesterday. I'm sure you'll be able to put them to good use."

"What is it?" I said.

P. J. opened the box.

"Wow!" she cried.

And "wow" was exactly right.

She picked out one of the neat, white, rectangular cards. The printing was sharp and clear. The artwork was perfect. This is how it looked:

P. J. CLOVER, Private

No case too large
No case too small
Stacy Jones, associate
phone 388–9456

Butch leaned over to look. "Far out," he murmured when he saw the card.

(And this time the look on his face was pure admiration.)

"Far out!"

P. J. beamed. She handed a card to Butch. "Keep it," she said graciously. "It may come in handy someday."

And with that, we swept into our office to wait . . . for our next case!

ABOUT THE AUTHOR

SUSAN MEYERS based P. J. Clover's detective agency on a crime-solving business that her daughter, Jessica, started when she was about P. J.'s age. The West Coast editor of *Enter* magazine, Ms. Meyers lives in San Francisco, California. She has written several other books for children, including P. J. CLOVER, PRIVATE EYE: *#2 The Case of the Missing Mouse*, and P. J. CLOVER, PRIVATE EYE: *#3 The Case of the Borrowed Baby*.